Sally Nicholls

Gosia Herba

The NOSE, TOES and TUMMY BOOK

Andersen Press

This is my **nose**.
What happens when I
press it?

BEEP!

This is your **nose**.
What happens when I
press your nose?

BEEP!

What a **noisy** nose!

These are your **ears**.

I like to whisper secrets in them.

"I just want to **gobble** you up!"

NOM-NOM-NOM-NOM-NOM-NOM-NOM!

And these are my **ears**.

What will you whisper to me?

This is my **mouth**.

I use it to **shout**.

ONE-
TWO-
THREE-

RRAAAWW

This is your **mouth**.

You can **shout** too.

ONE-
TWO-
THREE-

PRR!

RRAAAWWRR!

These are your **cheeks**.

This is my **face**.

Where's **my** face gone?

There it is!

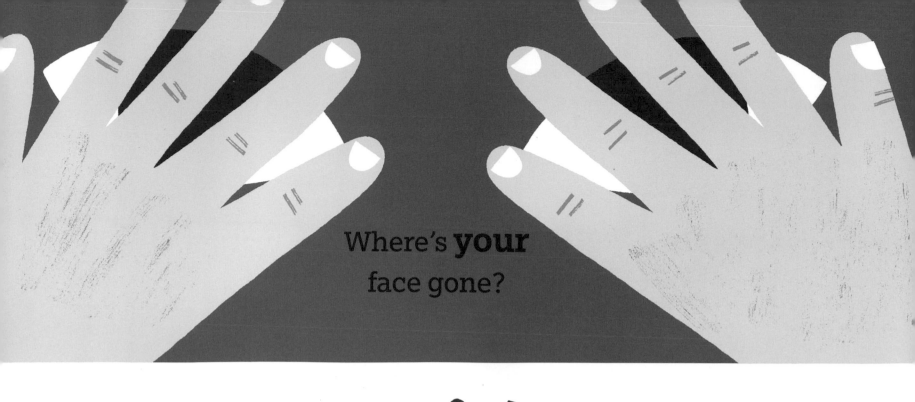

Where's **your** face gone?

There it is!

This is your **tummy**.

Who's got a tasty tummy?
You have!

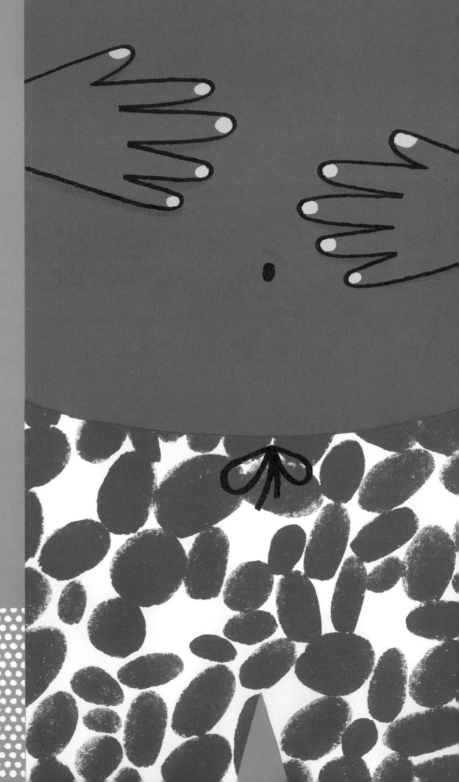

These are my **hands**.

My hands can **lift** you up in the air!

And now you're **upside** down!

What are you **doing** upside down?

You want to be the right way up! There! **That's better.**

SILLY HANDS!

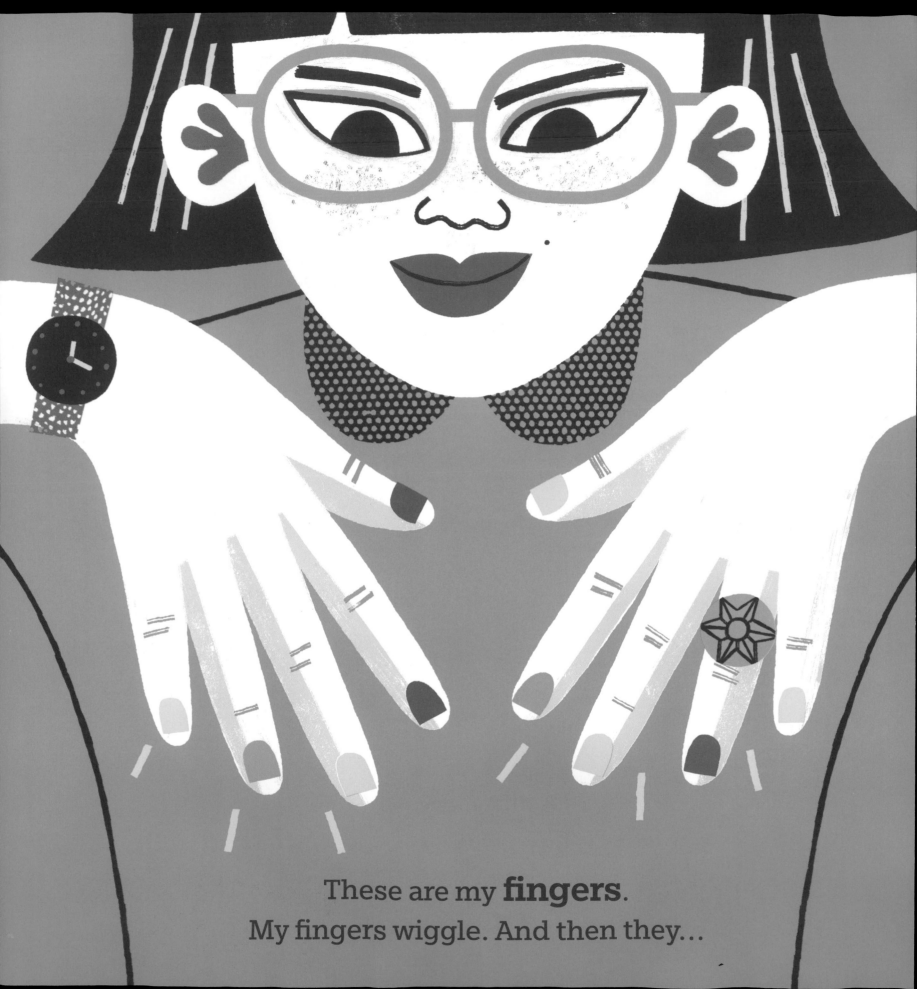

These are my **fingers**.
My fingers wiggle. And then they...

Now. These are my **legs**.

And these are your legs.

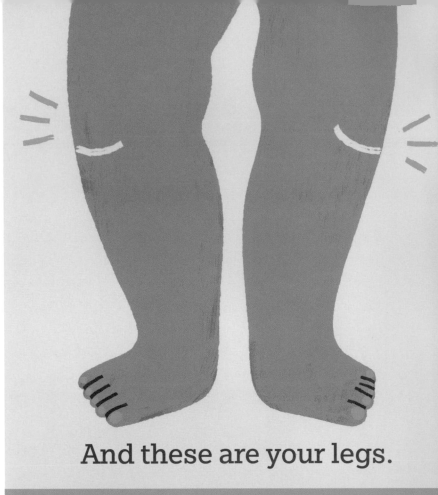

Legs go ROUND and ROUND.

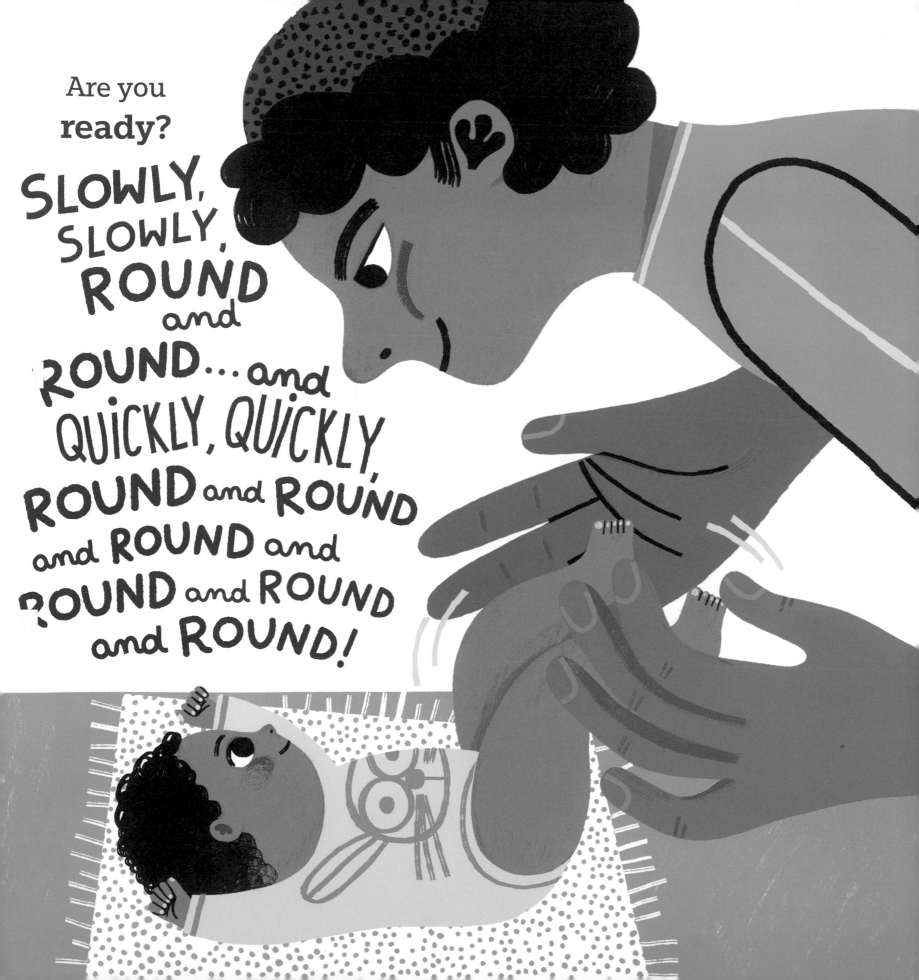

Are you **ready?**

SLOWLY,
SLOWLY,
ROUND
and
ROUND... and
QUICKLY, QUICKLY,
ROUND and ROUND
and ROUND and
ROUND and ROUND
and ROUND!

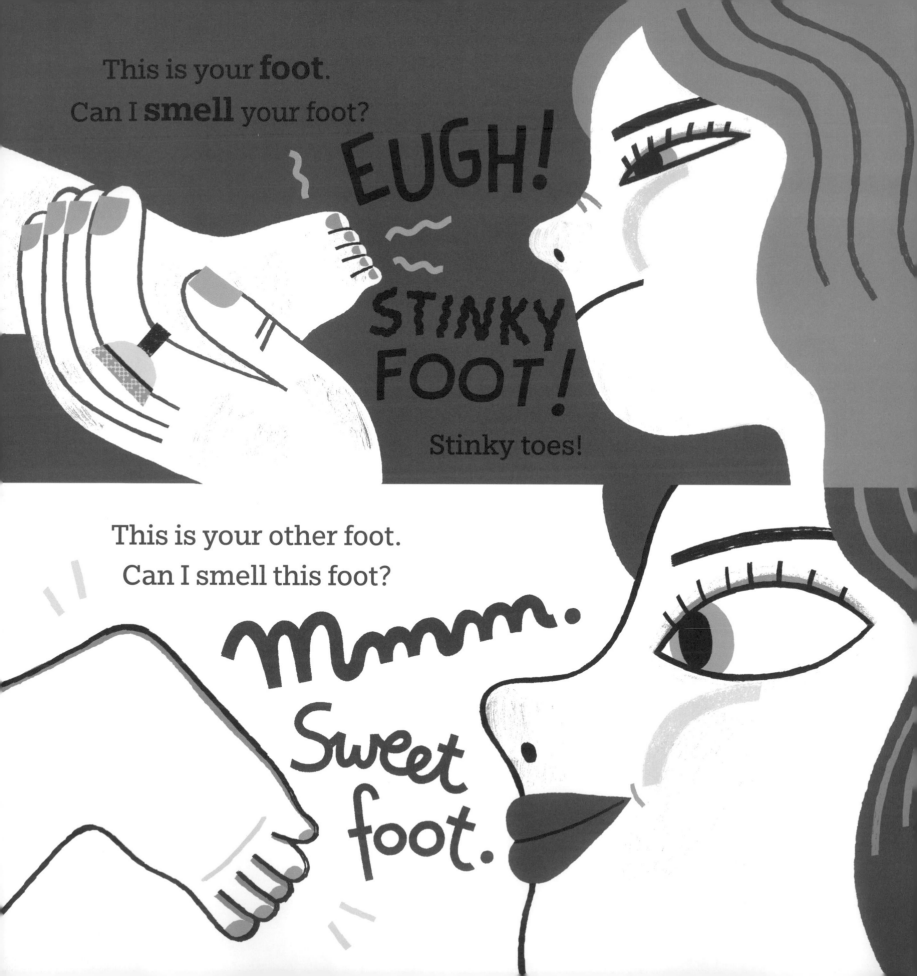

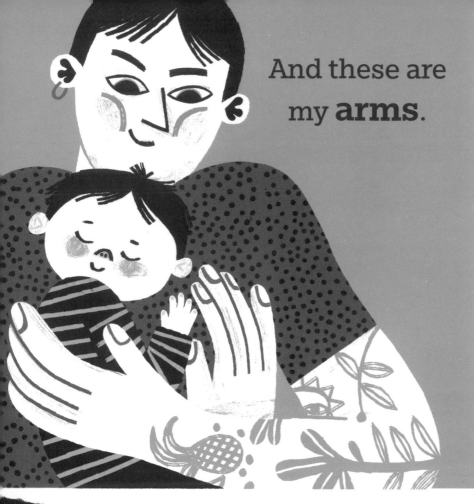

And these are my **arms**.

My arms hold you tight.

I **love** your **nose**, your **toes** and your **tummy**.

The top of your **head** and the bottom of your **feet**.